BENJAMIN'S LOST SOCK ADVENTURE

Written by: Melissa Schimke

Illustrated by: Lowell Hildebrandt

AuthorHouse™
1663 Liberty Drive
Bloomington, IN 47403
www.authorhouse.com
Phone: 1-800-839-8640

© 2012 Melissa Schimke. All rights reserved.

No part of this book may be reproduced, stored in a retrieval system,
or transmitted by any means without the written permission of the author.

First published by AuthorHouse 1/17/2012

ISBN: 978-1-4670-4469-1 (sc)

Library of Congress Control Number: 2011918369

Any people depicted in stock imagery provided by Thinkstock are models,
and such images are being used for illustrative purposes only.
Certain stock imagery © Thinkstock.

This book is printed on acid-free paper.

Because of the dynamic nature of the Internet, any web addresses or links contained in this book may have changed since publication and may no longer be valid. The views expressed in this work are solely those of the author and do not necessarily reflect the views of the publisher, and the publisher hereby disclaims any responsibility for them.

Benjamin woke up and stretched. Something was wrong. The sun was already shining through his window and mama always woke him up before it was light outside. He climbed out of bed and put on his school clothes, then went to his drawer to find some socks. He looked for his favorite blue pair but could only find one, so he pulled out some different socks, put on his right one and then his left one, being careful not to have the heel part on top. His shoes went on next; he put one shoe on then the other, tying them as tight as he could so they didn't untie.

Down the hall, Benjamin could hear his sister brushing her teeth, "brush, brush, brush…" he walked past the bathroom and down the stairs to the kitchen. Mama was always in the kitchen in the morning, but not today. Benjamin was confused. He walked into the living room and there she was with a big basket of clothes.

"I'm all ready for school mama," Benjamin said proudly.

"That's wonderful Ben, but there is no school today," said mama.

"There isn't?" Benjamin asked.

"No, there isn't. Today is a holiday and daddy and I have the day off of work too," mama replied. Benjamin sort of remembered his teacher telling the class to have a nice holiday weekend, but he hadn't paid much attention until now.

"Why is Jenny getting ready for school mama, she never brushes her teeth except on school days?"

Mama laughed.

"I am sure Jenny brushes her teeth all of the time Ben, you just don't notice. Jenny has been invited to a birthday party today, and daddy will be taking her there soon," mama replied.

"Can I go too?" Benjamin asked hopefully.

"No Ben it's a party for girls only!" Jenny said loudly as she walked into the room.

"Is not!" said Benjamin defensively.

"Is too!" exclaimed Jenny.

Mama broke in with a firm voice which said that was enough bickering.

"Mama, can I go too, please?" Benjamin pleaded, all the time glaring at Jenny.

"Not this time Ben, I need you here with me today. Daddy and I are catching up on some chores and I could use a good helper."

"Okay," said Benjamin in a deflated voice.

Mama looked at Benjamin.

"There will be times when you will get to go to birthday parties and Jenny won't," she said giving Jenny a smile when Benjamin's face brightened.

"Who would want to go to a boy's party anyway?" Jenny sneered and then said, "Mama, I finished cleaning my room like you told me to, and I'm almost ready to go, but I need my purple socks. Are they in the basket of clothes?"

Mama quickly sorted through the laundry and pulled out one purple sock. "Only one must have made it in this load Jenny, I'm sorry but you will have to wear some different socks," she said. Jenny huffed and stomped back up the stairs.

"Do you want some toast and juice Ben?" asked mama.

"Yes please" answered Ben. He was kind of hungry.

"Mama, where are the lost socks?" Benjamin asked later as he sat at the kitchen table eating his toast. Mama was just coming up the basement stairs with another basket of laundry. He remembered that one of his favorite blue socks was missing.

"Well, Ben that is a mystery that many people wonder about. Perhaps you can help me fold this basket of clothes and I'll tell you what I know about lost socks," said mama.

"Cool, I want to fold the towels!" Benjamin replied.

Mama smiled and went into the living room with the laundry. Ben finished his toast and juice, washed his hands and joined her a few minutes later, and mama began her story.

"Some people say that the socks disappear into a mysterious black hole in the universe to a place that only socks go I guess, but they must be able to go back and forth because they will sometimes just pop back up. Then, there are some socks that vanish and are never seen again, so wherever they go they must like it where they are and just stay."

Benjamin imagined a black hole where many different socks were running to and then jumping in. He pictured the other side of the black hole; a place where socks were having fun. Some socks were playing ball and others were riding bikes.

"Is it really true?" he asked.

"Well Ben, different people say different things, but one thing is for certain, everybody's house has a place where there are socks without matches. Sometimes it is a drawer, or a special basket like we have, or maybe a box, a bag, or shelf, and some people leave them in their laundry area just in case the match turns up."

Benjamin was intrigued. Now that he thought about it, he was always missing socks, and sometimes mama was able to go to that special small basket that had all single socks in it and find the one missing, but other times the other sock was no where to be found. He imagined socks trying to climb out of the special basket to get to the black hole in the universe. He began to fold the towels while he thought of the socks. Mama always gave him the towels because they were the easiest. First you folded them in half and then in half again. They started out as a big rectangle and then ended up as a square. The wash cloths were easy too and they made a little pile of small, colored squares next to Benjamin. Finally all that was left in the bottom of the basket were socks.

"Ben, would you start matching up the socks for me, while I go check on Jenny, please?" asked mama.

"Sure," said Benjamin.

He dumped the socks on the floor first and began to separate them like mama had showed him. He put the white ones in one pile and the colored ones in another pile. The colored socks were the easiest to match. There was Jenny's pink, short socks, and daddy's black ones and brown ones, which were medium length and mama had some long grey socks. Ben had some socks there too and among them was his missing blue sock.

"Hey!" He cried and ran up to his room. He opened his drawer and pulled out his other favorite blue sock, then rolled them together like mama had showed him. Benjamin smiled to himself and went back downstairs. Mama was matching socks and smiled at Benjamin.

"Look!" he said showing mama his blue socks. "I found one that was missing." He told her.

"Ahhh…" said mama mysteriously. "You must have had the match captured somewhere huh?" asked mama.

"Yes, in my drawer, how did you know?" He asked her.

Mama sighed, "Grandma used to tell me that if you had one, you better keep it where you could find it if the other one reappeared. She would take a clothespin and clip the single socks to a clothesline in our laundry room and sometimes they hung there so long without a match that she finally took them down."

"What did she do with them then?" Benjamin asked.

"Well, if grandpa had two that were close to matching, she would just put them together. She said that grandpa could wear them as 'work socks' and because he wore big boots, nobody would see them anyway."

Ben giggled as he thought of grandpa wearing mismatched socks.

Daddy came into the room. "Is Jenny almost ready to go?" he asked mama.

"Look daddy! I had one of my blue socks captured and now the match is back from the black hole in the universe," exclaimed Benjamin.

Daddy chuckled. "I see Ben. So you know about the back hole in the universe where all the socks go?"

"Yep, mama told me. You know about it too daddy?" asked Benjamin "Well, I didn't know about it until I met mama. My mama always told me that the Dryer Monster took the socks and kept them as pets. Sometimes he let them go, but his very favorites he always kept. The Dryer Monster can get into anybody's dryer even the public dryers and take the socks that he likes the best; he even takes socks from clotheslines when people aren't looking. Grandma Brigsby said the Dryer Monster can change sizes and be disguised as a ball of lint or a shriveled up dryer sheet," said daddy.

Ben tried to imagine what the Dryer Monster looked like. He thought of a big fluffy monster made of dryer lint that hid in the laundry, with huge eyes that could see in the dark. The dryer monster had hands that were kind of hairy and scratchy so when he reached into the dryer for the socks they just stuck to his sticky, hairy hands as they tumbled in the laundry. Ben noticed that socks would be stuck to dryer sheets when he dumped out  the baskets, maybe the Dryer Monster could leave his hands and get them later when no one was around.

"Wow!" exclaimed Benjamin. "Is that really what happens to the missing socks?" he asked.

"Ben, everyone knows that the washer eats the missing socks. Just ask Mrs. Thomas at school," said Jenny coming in on the conversation.

"I have heard that too," said mama, "but if the washer ate them Jenny why do they come back sometimes?" she asked.

"Because the washer doesn't like some of them and spits the socks back out," Jenny answered in a matter-of-fact voice.

Benjamin's mind was whirling. He started thinking about the big washer in the basement. He imagined it must have a huge long tongue that could wrap around the helpless socks as they swirled and swished in the water. When all of the other laundry was finished and removed then the washer would slowly swallow the poor socks. Benjamin wondered what the socks must taste like to the washer. Maybe they were flavored like colored candy was flavored. Jenny's purple socks must taste like grapes and daddy's brown ones like chocolate. Ben laughed out loud when he thought of mama's long grey socks. He had never eaten anything grey before, maybe they tasted like cement, or rocks, YUK!

"What's so funny?" asked Jenny

"I was just thinking about what the socks taste like," said Ben Jenny shook her head and rolled her eyes. "They don't taste like anything, Ben it's just a story made up to explain missing socks because no one really knows what happens to them."

"Time to go Jenny!" Daddy broke in with a grin.

Poor Benjamin, he just did not know what to believe. Benjamin decided he would ask his best friend Pete, who lived down the street. When daddy and Jenny left, he helped mama finish the laundry, and then asked if she would call Pete's mom to see if Pete could play.

"Sure," said mama. She dialed Pete's telephone number and talked with Pete's mom for a long time. She always did that when she called Pete's mom. Finally after what seemed to Benjamin a very long time, she said, "Pete's mom has some errands to run so she is bringing Pete over here to play. Is that okay with you?"

"I guess so," said Benjamin disappointedly.

"Well, that wasn't the response I was expecting Ben. What's wrong?" asked mama.

"I wanted to go to Pete's house to see his missing sock basket, and see what flavor socks were at his house, and ask him if he ever saw the Dryer Monster, or his hands anyway, or find out if maybe he ever heard the washing machine burp after the laundry was done, or saw the black hole in the universe at his house."

Benjamin was out of breath because it all came out in a big sentence. Mama looked at him as if he had turned into a monster himself, and then she laughed, but not at him, she laughed like she had heard a very good joke.

"Goodness you have quite an imagination! I know that you and Pete will have fun trying to solve the mystery of the missing socks."

Mama chuckled as she walked upstairs with the folded laundry. When she was half way up the stairs she paused and said "You know Ben, sometimes I find some of the missing socks just hiding in the strangest places throughout the house. I think maybe they are looking for the black hole in the universe, and don't know the way. Maybe you and Pete could go on a hunt for them and try to pair them up with their matches before they find it."

Ben's face lit up with enthusiasm.

"Yeah! That would be awesome!" Ben exclaimed. "I'll get all of the missing socks out so that we can see which ones we need to look for. Pete and I will find them all mama!"

"That's wonderful Ben," mama said as she finished walking up the stairs smiling.

Pete arrived soon after and Benjamin was excited to see his friend and tell him about the plan to find all of the missing socks. Pete listened as Benjamin told him everything he knew about lost socks and where the lost socks might be.

"But, what about the Sock Fairy?" Pete asked.

"The Sock Fairy? What is that?" asked Benjamin.

"My mom says it every time she is folding socks and there is one missing. She says: 'Well, the sock fairy has struck again.' Then she stuffs the socks without matches into a bag that she keeps by the washer. Once in a while she dumps out the bag and finds that there were matches in there all along, but there are always socks without any matches."

"But what does the Sock Fairy do with them Pete?" asked Benjamin.

"Awe, I don't know. My mom says she must make nice things with old socks." Pete sighed and shook his head.

Once again Benjamin's mind whirled as he imagined a beautiful fairy with wings and a magic wand taking the socks and making pretty sock flowers and sock pillows for the other fairies. "Well, I don't know about the Sock Fairy Pete. Maybe it's all true, and there are all of those different reasons why socks are missing,

but my mama says that sometimes she just finds the socks hiding and that they are lost or something. I told her we would go hunting and try to find all of our missing socks. Hey! Maybe we could go to your house too and find all of your missing socks!"

Pete shook his head sadly. Benjamin asked "What's the matter?"

"My mom took all of our socks without matches to a place where ladies make stuff out of them for sick kids. She says they're kind of like the Sock Fairy's helpers. She is going to buy us some new socks and we are starting over with all matching socks."

"Oh." said Benjamin. "That's okay we can still find our missing socks!"

"Okay!" Pete exclaimed.

Pete and Benjamin made a plan to start in Ben's room and began the search for the missing socks. Mama gave them each a flashlight and she took some old wire hangers and twisted them into a clever hook to "snag" the missing socks if they were in a hard to reach place. Mama said she would check on them later and announced that Pete would stay for lunch.

"Well, where do you want to start?" asked Pete

"Hmmm, this morning when I found my blue sock in the laundry I had the other one captured in my drawer. Maybe I have other ones captured too and don't know it!" said Ben.

They opened Benjamin's big dresser drawer where he kept his socks and started to look under the matched and rolled socks, t-shirts, and underwear. There was one old stained white sock that Benjamin remembered wearing while playing in the mud. The other one had a big hole in it and mama threw it away.

"This sock doesn't have a match anymore," said Benjamin. "Maybe your mom can take this one to those ladies."

"Sure," said Pete and he stuffed the sock in his pocket. "Should we look in your closet Ben?" asked Pete Benjamin looked at the closet door. He didn't like the closet very well. It was very dark, and the light switch was hard to reach.

Benjamin swallowed and said, "I guess so." They turned on their flashlights and opened the closet door. Benjamin's mind started thinking about the Dryer Monster and he swallowed again.

"I don't think there are any socks in here," he said to Pete.

"Wait!" said Pete. "I think I see something." Pete went further into the closet and Benjamin got a little nervous.

"What is it?" asked Benjamin

"I think it's a sock but it is stuck under the toy box," said Pete.

Benjamin was brave and went further into the closet to help Pete get the sock. He tried to lift the toy box while Pete pulled the sock out. When they shined the light on it, there stuck to the sock was an old dryer sheet. Pete and Benjamin both yelped, dropped the sock, and ran out of the closet.

"Do you really think that was the Dryer Monster's hand?" asked Pete.

"Maybe," said Benjamin. "We should get it and take it back to the basement. I don't want it in my closet."

"Awe, he won't hurt you Ben if he only likes socks. Let him have that old sock it looked too big to be yours anyway."

Benjamin agreed. The sock was a long white one with a red top. He remembered daddy playing tug-of war with Jack their dog using one that looked just like it only it had lots of knots tied in it. He remembered his dad saying that he couldn't find the other one so Jack could have the match to play with.

"The Dryer Monster was keeping daddy's sock all this time under my toy box." Benjamin told Pete. "I'll get it and show mama."

Benjamin opened the closet door and reached in with the long hook that mama made. He snagged the sock with the dryer sheet attached and carried it out in front of him. They walked downstairs and showed the sock to Benjamin's mom.

"Found one already?" she asked.

"Yep, and look what's on it mama!" Benjamin exclaimed.

"What, this?" she asked as she grabbed the dryer sheet off and threw it in the garbage.

"Mooommm!" Benjamin yelled. "That was the Dryer Monster's hand!"

"Oh my goodness Ben! You have quite an imagination," she said and smiled.

Pete just grinned, and Benjamin felt a little silly.

"Well I thought maybe it was," he said a little sheepishly.

"How about some lunch you guys" said Benjamin's mom. "Then you can search for Jenny's lost purple sock. We looked all over for it this morning. I sure hope that it didn't find the black hole in the universe," she smiled and winked at them both.

Benjamin brightened up and didn't feel so silly. He was hungry and his tummy made a growly noise when he thought of the food, and that also made him think of the washer downstairs.

"I think the washer was hungry and ate Jenny's sock mama. It must taste like grape because it's purple" he said.

Pete made a face. He didn't like grape candy, or grape juice.

"Hmmm now that is an interesting theory" said mama and she smiled again.

Benjamin and Pete ate the sandwiches that mama had made. They were very good and they drank all of their milk. Mama offered them a little more milk with two cookies each. Benjamin and Pete gobbled them up and drank the rest of the milk all the time talking about the search for Jenny's purple sock. Mama laughed out loud when Benjamin told Pete that they might have to hold their breath when they went into Jenny's room because it smelled funny.

"Well, it does." said Benjamin

Mama just smiled some more and shook her head. Benjamin didn't know why she always thought he said funny things.

"If you find Jenny's sock Ben, I am sure she will be so happy that she will give you a big hug. You too Pete," mama said smiling.

"Ewww YUK! You won't let her do that to us will you mama?" Benjamin asked hopefully.

Mama laughed again and took their empty milk glasses.

"Well if you don't want the hug Ben, I'm sure Jenny will just say thank you."

Benjamin didn't think Jenny would say thank you to him. She was always mean to him. But he was determined to find Jenny's purple sock anyway.

"C'mon Pete let's go up to Jenny's room," he said.

They grabbed their flashlights and their special "sock snaggers" then went back up the stairs to Jenny's room. Benjamin saw the sign on Jenny's door which was opened instead of closed like it normally was. He couldn't read it but he knew what some of the letters were. Jenny told him what it said one time when he asked her. Benjamin remembered her being mean again:

"It says:'NO BOYS ALLOWED'! And that means you!"

Benjamin told Jenny he didn't care, but he told mama anyway. He felt like Jenny was always too mean and she came into his room all the time, but mama didn't make her take down the sign which made him feel mad too. Benjamin smiled as he thought about going into Jenny's room. Mama was letting him and Pete go into her room now and boy would she be mad if she knew that. They went into Jenny's room. Mama had the shades pulled down to keep it cool so it was kind of dark in there. Jenny had a bed with big fluffy pillows on it and it smelled kind of sweet and kind of like that other stuff that mama and Jenny put on their fingernails. Pete wrinkled up his nose too.

"I told you so," said Benjamin when he saw Pete's face. Don't worry you'll get used to it."

Benjamin turned on his flashlight and began to look around. He remembered that Jenny was supposed to clean her room before the birthday party, but he knew that sometimes Jenny just kicked stuff under her bed.

"Pete let's look under Jenny's bed first. I don't think Jenny let mama look under there this morning." Ben said with an all knowing voice.

They shined their lights under the bed and noticed some different things: there was a book, some magazines, and a few articles of clothes but no socks. Next they looked behind Jenny's dresser but still no socks.

"Well, we could look in the closet, we found a sock in yours," said Pete.

Benjamin swallowed again and looked at Jenny's closet but he didn't want Pete to think he was scared. "Let's do it!" Benjamin said in a brave voice.

They went to the closet door which was halfway open and just as Pete grabbed the handle to open the door wider the door flew open on its own and a flash of grey fur came at them. Both Pete and Benjamin screamed and fell backwards and then laughed as Jack the dog began licking both of their faces.

"Jack! What are you doing in Jenny's closet?" Benjamin asked as he scratched Jack behind the ears. "Boy, you sure scared Pete!"

"He did not!" said Pete as he patted Jack. "I was just surprised that's all."

Pete spotted something in Jenny's closet and when he grabbed it Benjamin noticed that in Pete's hand was the missing purple sock.

"Hey! You found it!" exclaimed Benjamin, and then he noticed that Pete was holding it out and away from him.

"I know, Jenny's stuff smells bad," said Benjamin.

"No, it's not that Ben, I think Jack was chewing on it. It's all wet and sticky."

"Ewww!" said Benjamin. "Poor Jack! That must have tasted bad."

They took the sock downstairs to give to mama but she wasn't there. Benjamin heard her humming in the basement. He could also hear daddy

outside mowing the grass so he must have come back from taking Jenny to the party. Jack was eating and drinking from his dishes and Benjamin knew that Jack must have come inside when the lawn mower started. He didn't like the lawn mower. When Jack saw the purple sock he wagged his tail happily and barked at Benjamin. Mama came up the basement stairs.

"What's that about Jack?" asked mama as she smiled at him.

"He wants this!" said Benjamin as he held the sock out for mama. "Pete found it in Jenny's closet and it was all wet and slobbery." Pete nodded a confirmation.

"Bad dog Jack!" said mama, but Jack wagged his tail happily and went back to eating. Mama had her hands on her hips and shook her head. "I told daddy not to let Jack chew on socks. Jack doesn't know which ones are okay and which ones are not okay." She sighed and looked at the ruined purple sock. "Jenny is not going to be happy about this," she said.

"Maybe she can just wear two different socks like grandpa" Benjamin snickered and Pete giggled.

"I'm sure she will object to that!" said mama and laughed with them. "No, I will have to get Jenny another pair. These were her favorite socks."

"Hey! If I get Jack to chew on my bike can I get a new one?" asked Benjamin as Pete laughed again.

"Nice try pal, but I'm afraid not," said mama in a playfully firm voice.

Just then daddy came in from mowing the grass. Jack barked joyfully and went back out into the yard, very pleased that the mowing was over.

"Hi guys, what's going on?" daddy asked as he sat and wiped his brow. "Boy am I thirsty," he said as mama put a cold glass of iced tea in front of him.

"Mama is mad because you showed Jack how to chew on socks and he chewed up Jenny's purple one" said Benjamin.

"Oh, no." said daddy. "I found another sock in the yard while mowing and I threw it away. It was very dirty and full of holes where Jack chewed it." "But, I think I have an idea…" Daddy got up from the table and went out to the garbage. He pulled out the sock he found in the yard. "Where is Jenny's chewed up sock?" he asked. Mama gave it to him and he tied them together.

"Here," said mama. "The boys found this one underneath Ben's toy box." She handed daddy the sock with the red top. Daddy grinned.

"I think the other one to this has been Jack's chew toy for a while." Daddy went to Jack's doghouse and found the other sock. It was very dirty and chewed up with many holes next to the knots in it where Jack played tug-of-war with daddy. Daddy tied them all together and made many knots in them. Jack was watching him and barked happily when daddy showed it to him. "This is your toy now Jack, but no more good socks!" Jacked wagged his tail and barked again. "See?" He said to mama. "He won't chew any new socks. He understands, don't you boy?" Daddy patted Jack on the head and winked at Benjamin and Pete, as Jack played and shook the tied up, knotted, sock toy. Mama just rolled her eyes.

"He must be scolded if he does or he will do it again," said mama worriedly.

"Don't worry mama. We'll watch him close and make sure Jack isn't in our room when we leave." "You'll have to tell Jenny though because she won't listen to me!" said Benjamin.

"Well, this solves the mystery of these missing socks at least" mama said. "Have you found any non-chewed up socks?" she asked Benjamin and Pete.

"Not yet" said Benjamin, "but we will, huh Pete?" "Yep!" said Pete.

Benjamin and Pete grabbed up their sock hunting gear and headed upstairs again. They searched all of the rooms again and remembered to look under the beds and behind all of the doors. They had found two socks, one was one of daddy's but there was a very small red sock that was way too little for anyone in Ben's family. Pete gave Benjamin a puzzled look when they found it in mama and daddy's room. Benjamin thought about it and decided it must be his baby cousin's sock. They decided to go to the basement to see if the matches were in the basket. Mama had let Benjamin pull them all out and had helped him sort them by size and color. There were 22 socks in all, but none of them matched the two they had.

"We're just finding more matchless socks!" complained Benjamin. Pete just shook his head.

"You guys should start over like we did" he said. Benjamin placed the two socks with the rest.

"I don't get it," he said "where could they be?". Just then the washing machine began to shake and wobble and make a dreadful noise. Benjamin and Pete didn't know what to do. They watched as the washer moved from side to side as it began to move forward towards them.

"It's coming for the socks!" yelled Pete.

"Let's get out of here!" Benjamin yelled back.

"Goodness!" said Benjamin's mom appearing out of nowhere. She went over to the washer and lifted the lid. The washer slowly calmed.

"Be careful mama, it wants the socks" Ben said worriedly. Mama laughed again and said "Well I'm glad it is hungry for more laundry because we have plenty. It was out of balance Ben, which sometimes happens if the laundry is wet and heavier on one side than the other. It makes a terrible racket when that happens." Benjamin and Pete watched as Benjamin's mom rearranged the laundry then close the lid on the washer. It began to spin again smoothly and quietly.

"Hey I see that you found baby John's, red sock" said mama.

"That is John's?" asked Benjamin

"Yes and Aunt Hillary will be glad you found it. We couldn't seem to find it last weekend when they visited." said mama

"Why did Aunt Hill let baby John go in the hall closet upstairs?" asked Benjamin.

"Well I'm quite sure she didn't Ben. Why?" asked mama a bit confused.

"That's where we found baby John's red sock." said Pete then he laughed out loud.

"What's so funny?" asked Benjamin.

"You called baby John's mommy 'ant hill'." Pete replied. "It's sort of funny!"

Mama smiled again and shook her head.

"You guys are jokers today." she said.

Benjamin laughed too. He thought Pete was clever.

"Mama how did baby John's sock get in the hall closet if he wasn't in there. Do you think that is where the black hole in the universe is?"

"I just don't know Ben." mama answered. "Socks have been going missing for as long as I can remember, and as I said before, I always find socks in the strangest places." Mama shook her head and then said, "I came down to say that Pete's mom is done with her errands and wants to take you two for ice cream. She will be here soon, so if would like to go you should wash your hands and put away your things. I will take care of the flashlights if you guys want to take your sock grabbers to the shed outside."

"Yes!" cried Pete and Benjamin together.

They quickly did as mama said and pretty soon Pete's mom came to get them. Later over ice cream they told Pete's mom all about the big sock adventure they had and everything they thought about the lost socks. Pete's mom laughed very loud at some of the parts, just like Mama laughed, and shook her head too like she heard a very funny joke.

When Benjamin got home, he saw Jenny playing with Jack and his new sock toy. She didn't seem mad at all, and she even smiled and waved at him. Benjamin was surprised, but that wasn't all! Jenny brought home an extra balloon from the birthday party. He just couldn't believe it!

After supper, while mama was cleaning up supper and daddy helped with the dishes, Benjamin and Jenny went back outside to play with Jack again Benjamin didn't know what to say to the strange, nice Jenny so he said thanks for the balloon.

"You're welcome Ben. "Ann's mom said I should bring you one because there were so many. Besides, mama said you looked very hard for my purple sock and found it."

"But aren't you mad that it's ruined?" he asked

"I was at first, but mama said we could go get a new pair and secretly I have wanted a new pair of purple socks." Jenny said in a low voice smiling.

"Jenny, do you know what really happens to the lost socks?" Benjamin asked his sister.

"Not really. They just get lost Ben, no one really knows, not even mama and daddy." "Ann said they have lots of lost socks too. Maybe if everyone put their single socks together we would find matches" she said laughing.

"Maybe." said Benjamin grinning. "Mama said we have to watch Jack close though."

"She told me too," said Jenny. "I have to keep my door shut tight, and mama said to tell you it's not because of you, it's because I have to keep Jack out."

That night as Benjamin was getting ready for bed; he took off his socks and placed them both together in his dirty clothes bin. He thought about them for a long time and wondered if one of them would try to find the black hole in the universe, or get snatched up by the Dryer Monster, taken by the Sock Fairy, or swallowed up by the washer. Benjamin was still determined to find out more about the lost socks and if other people had ideas about them.

Now that the holiday was over, Benjamin was excited to share his lost sock holiday adventure with his other friends at school tomorrow.

Benjamin climbed under the covers and lay down with his hands behind his head, staring up at his ceiling, and as his thoughts began to drift he thought:

'They're out there somewhere!'

CPSIA information can be obtained
at www.ICGtesting.com
Printed in the USA
274527LV00001B